HARD AS WOOD

A PUPPET LOVE STORY

G.M. FAIRY

Content Warning

Hard as Wood is not suitable for all readers.

For a full list of content warnings, please visit

gmfairyauthor.com

Chapter One
CLARA

Surrounded by people, and yet I always feel alone. As I push through the bustling cobblestone streets, I curse myself for forgetting the midday rush when deciding to leave for the market. A tall man elbows me in the nose, and when I cry out, he barely gives me a sideways glance. I huff, holding my burlap sack closer to my chest and slipping through the cracks of people so I can walk on the outskirts of the walkway. That's the third person to accidentally assault me in the last five minutes. It's getting ridiculous.

It's always like this. I'm invisible even if I'm not in a crowd. Of course, my build is partially to blame, considering I'm five feet one and barely occupy space. I grew up feeling cursed, but my father told me that most people are too caught up with themselves to see what's right in front of them. I'd do anything on days like these to hear my father's sweet voice again.

I sigh and turn off the pathway, deciding that the rest of my errands can wait for a less busy time. Luckily, there's a route home through the woods. It will take longer, but I don't mind being alone with nature. I'm always alone. At least in these woods, I can hear the birds and rustles of creatures around me.

It takes me thirty minutes to glimpse my squatty wood cabin in the distance. My heart sings once she comes into view—the home my father built for us—one of the few things I have left of him.

As I push through the oak door, I'm greeted by the scent of the fresh bread I baked this morning. "I'm home!" I sing, placing my sack on the table and pulling out the new set of paints I picked up. "Oh, Molly. I forgot to get buttons for the sweater I'm knitting you. I'll have to pick them up when I return later this week." I walk to the large shelves adhered to the wall, parallel to the windows overlooking the outside greenery.

"Pineo, I have a surprise for you." I pull the small canister of green paint and the fine-tipped brush from behind my back. "I told you I'd get that eye taken care of." I lean forward with a steady hand, placing a small dot of green paint on the chip in his eye. "There, all better!" I exclaim, placing my hands on my hips and stepping back to look at my work.

Pineo sits at the center of the shelves, his two eyes back to their matching joyous glow. All around him are other wooden puppets of various shapes, sizes, and species—all beautifully crafted and intricate. But Pineo has always been my favorite.

It's safe to say that these puppets are my only friend. My father crafted each one with love and care before he passed away five years ago. They've always held a special place in my heart, but now that I'm alone, their spot is even wider. Besides my chores, taking care of my puppets consumes all my time, but I always make sure to give Pineo a little bit more of me.

When I was five, my father surprised me with Pineo. He performed plays for me using a wooden box as a stage. Pineo was the Prince Charming. My father never crafted me a princess. He always told me there was no need for two princesses in his kingdom. Almost twenty years later, I still view Pineo as my prince. I know he's not a real man and will never be—I haven't fallen that crazy yet. But I like to keep him as the archetype. If a man doesn't live up to Pineo's standards, he doesn't cut it.

Who am I kidding, though? It's not like there's a line of men outside just waiting for their chance to date the mousy brunette who still plays with dolls. It's fine with me, though. My puppets serve as much better company than the smelly, pushy men I've had the pleasure of meeting in town.

However, sometimes, an urge takes over me on a cold and rainy night. I think of the fairytales I grew up reading and imagine what happens after the big true love kiss. What does it look like when the prince sweeps the princess off her feet and brings her back to his castle? I've never been with a man, but I've seen the dirty pictures hidden behind the town bookstore. I've witnessed couples embracing in alleys in the dead of night, their hands lingering in forbidden places. I may dislike men, but I wouldn't mind being touched like that—in the way my fingers dance across my skin when my loneliness takes hold of me.

I spend the rest of my evening sipping tea by the fire, looking out at the forest as the sky grays and opens up, gradually turning into a heavy rain. The cold seeps in, beating the fire's attempts, and I curl up with an old quilt, glancing at my wooden puppets. Pineo's eye catches my attention.

I sure did a good job repairing his eye. He's so handsome, even as a wooden doll. He has a strong jaw, a large nose, and his brown horsehair just grazes his painted-on eyebrows. If he was a human, he'd be my type. I stand, holding my quilt around my shoulders, grab Pineo off the shelf, and kiss his wooden face before placing him back in his spot. "Oh, Pineo. If only you were real. I know you wouldn't ignore me. I'm sure of it." I shuffle back to my spot in my chair and lie down, capturing his wooden eyes across the room. There's always been something about them, even when he had the chip. It's why he's my favorite.

The rain subsides, and I turn to look out the window. The sky clears, and bright stars shine through the black. One star stands out amongst the rest, bright and beautiful. My eyes droop as I stare at the light. "Oh, I wish Pineo was real," I mutter as my consciousness blinks out, my dreams of my wooden man already pulling me under.

Chapter Two

PINEO

My awareness opens as a rooster calls in the distance. Something flutters against my face, startling me, but the thought dulls in comparison to the view before me. Was I moved in the night? The room doesn't look like it did when I fell asleep. Everything is smaller—the proportions way off.

My beautiful Clara still sleeps on the chair near the window, calming my initial nerves for her safety. Her chest rises and falls, and a soft smile splays over her face as the early morning sunlight illuminates her features. Her brown wavy hair hangs off the cushion along with her outstretched arm. Ever since my creation twenty years ago,

Clara has been the reason for my existence. I'm just a wooden doll—a plaything, but every fiber of my being buzzes for her attention.

I often wonder if the other wooden dolls around me feel the same. We can't communicate. I can't open my eyes or mouth or move, but the thought that Sam or Emily might feel the same way I feel fills me with rage. Sometimes, I wish Clara would get rid of all the other puppets so that I could consume her attention. Whenever I think the thought though, I reprimand myself. The other puppets bring Clara joy. I'd never want to take any ounce of happiness away from her.

The flutter happens again, and I startle—actually startle, my body shaking and hitting the wall behind me. I bring up my hand to my face, feeling my eyelashes flick against my palm. Wait. I brought my hand up to my face? I scream, the deep sound startling me even more and making me tumble off my shelf and onto the floor below me.

I'm in a heap on the ground as Clara's screams ring around me. I jump to my feet. "My Clara, what is wrong? I will protect you?" These are words I've always wanted to say. Clara's sweet name whisps across my lips, and I want to bite my tongue just to taste the word again.

"Who are you? Get out of my house!" she yells.

I look around, ready to attack whoever she is referring to. I'm not registering that I can talk, stand, or move; I'm thinking about how to protect my love.

A pillow hits my head, and I turn back to Clara. She's jumped onto the chair, another plush pillow coiled back in her arm, ready to be thrown. I capture her eyes with mine—her rich brown irises sucking me in. My shoulders sag, and something twitches in my pants as I gaze at her, making me forget my mission of protecting.

"What are you looking at?" she barks, fear strewn across her face. "What do you want from me?"

It's me. She's afraid of me. I don't understand. She's always told me I'm her favorite, given me the most attention, and watched me as her fingers dived beneath her skirts and moans bellowed from her mouth. What has changed?

As if she can read my thoughts, she asks, "Why do you look confused? Did you stumble into the wrong house or something?" Her expression changes from petrified to concerned. My sweet girl, always caring for others first.

I look down, shocked to find my body has changed. Well, actually, I'm shocked I can even look down. I raise my arm, bringing it to my line of vision. "I can move," I say in awe. "And I've grown." My voice startles me again, strong and deep. I cover my mouth with my hands.

Clara squints at me, dropping her pillow and stepping closer. She examines me slowly before her eyes widen, and she snaps her attention to the shelves behind me. She runs to the empty spot in the middle before turning to me. "Pineo? Is that you?"

"Yes, it's me." I place my hand on my chest, stepping toward her—my drive to get closer overtaking the shakiness of my legs.

"How is this possible?" Her eyes dart to every inch of me.

I don't waste a second, removing the space between us and wrapping her into my arms. Her arms connect around my neck, and my hands scoop under her, lifting her from the ground and spinning her softly. Her heart hammers against my chest. "Am I dreaming? What's going on?" She's trying to put the pieces together when I couldn't care less. All I care about is that she's in my arms, and I can finally communicate with her.

She pushes away and makes herself heavier as an indication to place her back on the floor. I do, but my face droops that she already needs her space. Her hands remain on my chest, feeling up my green vest. "Your clothes, they grew too." Her hands travel to my neck and to my jawline. "But you're still made of wood. You're a wooden person. How is this possible?"

I wrap my fingers around her wrists, staring into her brown eyes, catching my reflection. I look the same: wooden features, green eyes, and wavy blonde horsehair adhered to my head, but I'm much bigger, towering over my Clara. I study her face. She wants answers, and she's looking to me to give them to her. I clear my throat. "Maybe it was your wish last night. You wished on a star to make me real," I offer.

Clara nods, brightness filling her expression. "Yes, I did wish on a star. It's just like the storybooks." She smiles. "And you're my prince charming come to life."

My wooden heart elates at her words. "You've always been my princess." An urge takes over me, something natural but foreign. I lean in, wanting her mouth against mine. She startles at first, but her lips part, and she rises on her tip-toes, closing the distance between us and bringing her soft lips to my wooden ones. Electricity zips through my body, and my knees grow weak. I press in deep, and her tongue reaches into my mouth. I open wide, letting her explore, as I match her languid movements. A soft moan escapes her as she holds onto me tightly, her body rubbing against my front.

She pulls back, her eyes wide as if a thought just popped into her mind. "Did you watch me all those nights when...you know?"

I study her, not sure what she means.

Her cheeks redden, and her eyes dart nervously. "When I...touched myself, down there." She motions with her eyes. "And I would cry out in pleasure. Did you watch?"

My heart beats thunderously. I always watched Clara, no matter what she did, but my favorite time of all was when she touched herself between her legs. She would glue her eyes to me, not breaking her gaze even as her body convulsed under her touch. I didn't know exactly what was happening, but it stirred something in me. She never touched herself like that when anyone else was home. She always closed the blinds and double-checked to ensure no one was watching her. Obviously, this was a private act she didn't want anyone to see. I don't want to scare her away. "No," I lie, immediately regretting my choice.

Something like disappointment flashes across her face. I don't have time to ponder it because my body grabs my attention. My plaid pants tent, growing tighter until something bursts through the seam.

Clara gasps, looking down at the strange wooden rod protruding through my pants. "Is that your...?"

I look back and forth between her and my strange body part. "I think it's my penis," I say. I've never had a penis before, but I guess now that I'm a human, I do. New information rushes through my brain. No one has ever told me the purpose of this body part, but some new instinct rests inside of me. "Do they usually grow when you tell a lie?" Maybe I don't know everything about my penis.

She giggles, covering her mouth with her hand. "Did you just lie?" My long penis separates us now. I hate the thing. Why is it creating distance between my sweet Clara? It also throbs and makes my body feel strange.

I nod. "Yes. I'm sorry. I said I haven't watched you touch yourself, but I always watch you. It's one of my favorite things you do."

Her smile fades, and her lips part. I must have upset her. Now I hate my penis and my mouth. Maybe I'm not cut out for my new body.

"Why did you lie to me?" Her voice is heavy and shaky.

"I didn't want to upset you. I'm sorry. I shouldn't have watched you all these years."

"Don't say that." She moves around my penis and places her hand on my chest. My body ignites under her touch, and my penis twitches. Stupid penis.

"I want you to watch me." She stands on her tip-toes and nuzzles into the crook of my neck. My shoulders sag at her heavy breath on my wooden skin, and my penis aches even more. Something drips from the tip. My eyes widened as I look at the amber-colored gel from afar. Great, now my penis is also disgusting.

Clara must notice my sudden shock from the stiffness of my body. Her eyes follow my gaze, and she leaves my side, stepping in front of my very long wooden member. She swipes her finger in the substance, bringing it to her lips. The small contact from her finger elicits a rush of pleasure from the base of my spine. Okay, maybe my penis isn't so bad.

Her eyes grow wide in delight. "It tastes like maple syrup." She licks her finger again as if to get off every last drop. I have half a mind to let her know that the heavy feeling in my wooden testicles might indicate there's a lot more where that came from.

Oh yeah. I guess I have testicles now. That's new. I don't know what they do or how they work, but I feel it won't be too hard to find out. I thank the Maker for the sprinkles of knowledge about my new body encoded in my wooden brain. I'm confused about a lot of things, but I'm grateful I at least know some things about my genitals.

"I've heard girls at the market talk about their husbands' cum and say it tastes horrible. Yours doesn't taste bad at all. It's delicious." Clara lowers to her knees, eye level with my rod.

I only started breathing a few minutes ago but suddenly forget how to do it. "What are you doing?" I ask. I'd let Clara do whatever she deems fit. If she wanted to chop me up into a million tiny toothpicks, I wouldn't resist. Her whim is my fancy. I only ask now as I have a creeping suspicion she's about to put her mouth on me, and I want to visualize it even for just a second so I don't succumb to the bubbling pressure building in my abdomen. My penis feels dangerous.

"I want to make you feel good," she purrs before opening her mouth and wrapping her full lips over my head.

Her mouth is on my penis. Her mouth is on my penis.

She swallows me, taking me in until I hit the back of her throat, and she gags.

Oh, Maker, I love my penis. I officially love my penis.

She pulls away, strings of saliva connecting me to her mouth. "I can't take your whole cock. It's too big."

"My cock?" I get out with a pained whine. The absence of her heat on me is too much to bear. I hold onto the wall next to me to regain balance. I'm thankful she pulled away, though. That building pressure is becoming increasingly intense, and I have no idea what will happen next.

She giggles, her smile so magnetic that just the sight of it pulls a groan from my throat. "That's what some people call a penis. It used to sound crude to me, but I like saying it now." As she talks, she rolls her hand down my *cock*, using her saliva as the lubricant. I can't focus on her words when she does that. I close my eyes, my vision turning blurry.

"You can call me or my body anything you want, especially if you keep touching me like that." My voice shakes.

"You like this?" Her strokes lower to as long as her arm will stretch.

"Maker, yes." I can barely hold myself upright. Something builds inside of me. I have only felt a few things in my recent period of being alive, but this feels powerful—even for a human. It scares me like my insides are about to explode, and I have no control. Clara seems to know what she's doing—it sure feels like it. I only hope that she doesn't let this be the end of me. Although, I wouldn't mind ceasing my time alive like this.

She returns her lips to my cock, continuing her strokes. In only a few seconds, a powerful force takes hold of me again. "Oh no!" I yell. I'm scared, but Maker, I've never felt better. It's like every happy thought in the world exists in my body. I can't control myself. Something shoots out from my wooden member; I imagine it's the "maple syrup" substance from before. As I suspected, it feels like a lot. I'm horrified at myself, but I watch in awe as Clara moans and gulps it down. Her hand is tucked into her underwear, moving frantically. She's touching herself as she swallows my liquid. Whatever is happening right now is arousing her.

She doesn't remove her lips from me until my penis slowly shrinks, moving closer to my body. Her breath heavies and her hand remains up her skirt and down her underwear. I drop to my knees, grabbing her arms. "What did you do to me?" I ask, mystified, examining her as if she holds the world's magic in her touch.

Her eyes shoot open. "Did you like it? I'm sorry. I should have asked and made sure it was okay with you."

I grab her, cradling her in my arms as if she's a doll and I'm a human. "That was the most wonderful thing I ever experienced. I can't thank you enough."

She laughs, her hand on my chest. "It's just a blow job, and it's the first one I ever gave. I doubt it was that good."

I shake my head and keep my eyes locked with hers. "That was not *just* anything. If people knew that you could elicit that kind of pleasure, they'd be lining out the door for your blow jobs!"

She laughs and slaps my chest. "No! You don't give out blowjobs to just anyone. It has to be with someone special that you like romantically." She scrunches her forehead and looks up as if in thought. "Well, I guess that's not always true, but at least it is for me."

"You like me romantically?" I ask with a smile.

Her cheeks redden, and she grins—wide and beautiful. I wish I could catch the sight of her like this forever. "Yes.

I've always liked you a little more than I should like a wooden doll."

"I can't tell you how happy that makes me."

"Oh, Pineo!" She wraps her arms around my neck and places her lips on mine. This isn't the first time she's kissed me. She would put her lips on me like this when I was a puppet, but I can kiss back this time. I hold her closer to me, slipping my tongue into her mouth and tasting the inside of her. She's the first thing I've ever tasted, but I already know it will be the sweetest. I wish to taste all of her.

She moans into my mouth. My cock twitches. I pull back, looking down at my wooden friend. He hasn't grown this time. Well, that's not true. His little wooden head pokes out from the hole he made in my pants, but he's not nearly as long as before. My body is confusing. I'm thankful I get to explore it with Clara.

Clara grabs my head, turning it back to her and placing her lips on mine. She kisses me with a deep hunger and makes noises like when she touched herself and I would watch from my shelf or the corner of her room.

I wonder if she'd let me touch her like that. She did just touch me and put her lips on my cock. I hope she'll let me do the same. As much as it pains me, I pull back from her lips and look around the living room. All the windows are open, and even though I can't see anyone through them, I don't want to risk it.

I walk down the hallway to her room, still holding her in my arms. "Where are we going?" she asks.

"I'd like to touch you, and I don't want anyone to see. I don't know why, but the thought of it makes my stomach flip."

She laughs, gazing at me, her fingers locked in my hair. "It's called jealousy."

"Well, I hate it." I've felt the feeling as a puppet, but now I have a name for it.

"Don't worry, you don't need to be jealous. I'm all yours. I've always been yours."

Her words warm my insides. We're in her room, and I shut the door behind me. I've been here many times, but it looks so different from my new proportions. I don't have time to take in everything, though. I have a woman to please.

I place her on her bed gently. She closes her eyes and arches her back. I'm frozen. Maker, she's beautiful. Her full breasts spill to her side, her brown hair mixing with her earth-colored quilt—I could stare at her all day. I've already witnessed her pleasure before, alone and far away on my shelf. Now I'll be able to see up close. I can barely wait another second.

I fold over her, kissing down her neck. "Oh, Pineo." She moans, running her fingers through my hair. I bring my lips to her ear. "I want to make your lips part around a perfect moan. I want to see you lost in pleasure under my touch."

"I've never had someone touch me like that before," she whispers.

I hold myself up on my elbows, capturing my eyes with her. "And I've never touched anyone, so we'll explore this new journey together. I've spent many nights watching your fingers dance between your legs. I'm certain I can move just the way you like." I know her expression so well. She bites her lip, and I can tell she's nervous, but from the rosy blush on her cheeks and the way her eyes seem electrified, she's excited about what's about to happen.

I keep my eyes locked on hers as I slide up her leg and under her full skirt. She's so warm and soft, and I nearly melt into her. I continue to move higher until I reach the apex of her thigh. It's warmer here, nearly scorching, and my fingers seek out the source of the heat.

She gasps as I graze the outside of her lips, the beautiful peach skin that folds into her core. I've watched her massage herself here many times. The air would thicken with a sweet smell, her breath heavied, a wet sound flooded my ears, her eyes closed, and she strummed herself with an easy tempo until she cried out in a glorious pitch. Here I am, right at the source of so much euphoria—right at the place I've always dreamt of.

I push my finger in more, softly and slowly. She gasps, her nails cutting into my wooden back. "Tell me if it's too much," I whisper.

"Pineo, it's so good. Oh, God, it's so much better than I could ever imagine."

I'm barely even touching her. My finger just dipped in her wetness. I've never been able to feel her before, but I'm sure that this is the wettest she's ever been. I imagine my wooden cock could slide right into her. It's like her body was made for me—as if a divine Maker made her as well.

I stroke up and down her slickness, moving easily. She feels so good under my touch, and I moan. "Does this feel good?" I ask.

"Oh, yes. Pineo. Too good."

"It feels good for me too. I think that sticky stuff might erupt from me again."

"Oh God, that's so hot!"

Her breath is heavy—like the weight of when she's about to scream out, but I just started. I don't want the fun to end yet. I move down her until I reach her entrance. I watched her dive her fingers into herself, wishing that was me filling her. Now, I slowly stick one finger inside of her. She clenches around me and cries out. "Oh, my God!"

I don't know who this *God* is, but I'm awfully tired of hearing his name coming from her mouth. I lean in to her ear. "I only want to hear my name on your lips. I'm the one who's filling you, not God." I don't mean to be aggressive, but something comes over me when seeing her like this. My cock is longer than before, but not as long as it was minutes ago, and it's like it has a mind of its own—begging me to insert myself into her, to claim her, to never let her go.

She grabs my face, looking into my eyes. "Yes, Pineo. Only you." Something settles inside of me. I'm sated partially. "Good, girl," I whisper, continuing to insert one finger while I play with her bundle of nerves at the top of her sex.

"Yes, Pineo! Just like that!" she cries.

I knew she'd like it like this. I've always been a good student; now is my time to shine. It usually takes her a while to finish her pleasure, but I'm confident I can make her reach her edge soon. Not that I want this to end. No, I wish this could last forever, but I bet there are a lot more touching sessions in store for us.

I increase my speed, applying the perfect amount of pressure.

"Oh, my! Pineo! Why are you so good at this?" she's panting over her words. "Fuck! That's so good! I'm coming. I'm coming!"

"Yes, you are." I kiss her temple as she convulses in my arms, and I loom over her. Her body turns as rigid as my wooden cock. She arches her back, and now I'm moaning—watching as she melts under my fingers. My insides are mush again, and I erupt. Thankfully, it's not as intense this time because I want to study Clara. I've never seen something so powerful come from her, and I want to remember every moment.

I'm still strumming her, and she continues to rock against my fingers. One of her hands brushes in the syrup dripping out of the hole of my pants. She gasps, twirling her fingers in the substance and bringing it to her lips. "Oh, you came, Pineo. Such a good boy." She moans. I like being called a good boy. It makes my cock grow again.

I continue to move in her juices until her body slacks, and she stills, catching her breath. I kiss every inch of her face and nuzzle next to her.

"I still don't know if I'm dreaming," she finally whispers after a moment of silence has passed.

I bury my head in the crook of her neck, soaking in the smell of the fresh sweat on her skin. "If this is a dream, I don't want to wake up."

Chapter Three

CLARA

I tried to stay up as long as I could. Even though my body felt like a tub of melted butter, and I couldn't remove myself from the tangle of Pineo's wooden arms, I did my best to keep myself awake. Pineo fell asleep quickly after he touched me to completion, and I watched him, studying the way his chest rose and fell. As weird as it sounds, I thought of my father. He made Pineo when I was a little girl. Maybe he sent magic from heaven down to Earth to turn him into a real man just for me. It was a comforting thought.

I couldn't keep my hands off him as I snuggled close, tracing the grain lines on his arms and over his cheeks.

I was mesmerized by him, a living, breathing, life-sized wooden man. My fascination with his form couldn't keep my eyelids from drooping, though. My body felt too good and drifted off to a restful slumber.

Now, I'm afraid to open my eyes. Afraid that Pineo won't be lying next to me and that everything that happened was just a dream. I can't lie here forever, though. The rumbling in my stomach won't allow it. I open my eyes and turn to the spot next to me—the spot Pineo lay as he ran his wooden fingers down my cheek while I fell asleep. Except now it's empty.

Tears form in the corner of my eyes. Of course, it was only a dream. This is the real world where puppets don't turn into men, and young women who dream about falling in love with toys become lonely spinsters.

A bang sounds from my kitchen. I've never been so happy to hear the clattering of pans. I jump from my bed, pull a blanket around me, and shuffle out of my room. Pineo stands at the stove, hands on his hips as he looks down at a pan.

I rush toward him, wrapping my arms around his middle and resting my head on his back. He rubs my hands on his chest. "Good morning," he says, turning and kissing me on the lips. I kiss him back, less gentle than him, darting my tongue into his mouth. I'm just so happy he's here and not a figment of my imagination. He returns my hunger tenfold, grabbing my face and deepening our embrace. Yes, I'm starving, but his wooden lips elicit a deeper hunger. Fooling around was magical and perfect and everything I dreamed of, but I want more. I want his long wooden dick pounding inside of me, especially when it grows as long as it did yesterday, even if it's dangerous.

My hands trail down his torso, fumbling over his crotch. "Oh no," I pull away, looking at the torn fabric. "Your pants are still ripped." I fall to my knees, assessing if I can sow the hole myself. His wooden nob pokes out.

"Clara, seeing you on your knees like this is too much, too early."

I look up. His eyes are clenched, and I chuckle, pushing back up to my feet. "I don't mind getting on my knees for you early in the morning."

He holds my shoulders, pushing me back a smidge. "Yes, but you need to eat first. I can't have you withering away on me."

My stomach grumbles on cue. I sigh. "Okay, fine. Real food first." I move around him, glancing at the two unbroken eggs on the unlit stove top. "Um, do you need help?"

His cheeks blush, and he drops his eyes to his feet. "It seems cooking is one of the many things I don't know how to do."

I wrap my arms around his neck, pulling his cheek to my lips. "It's okay. It's only your first day. Besides, there's one thing I know that you're excellent at," I whisper into his ear.

He moans, digging his fingertips into my backside.

I pull back before my desire washes over me, preventing any other tasks from happening today. I pat his chest. "Let's go into town. We can get you new pants and pick up something to eat. You've never eaten food before. I think your first time should be something amazing." I can't help but think how I want my first time—not eating, but something that will bring me even more pleasure—to be amazing too. I want it to be with Pineo, but don't want to rush. I want us to both be rested, full and ready to exert as much energy as it takes until we're sated, and judging by the need rushing through my body, it will take a while.

Pineo nods with a smile. "Is it okay to go out like this?" He looks down at the hole in his pants.

I tap my lip, glancing around the kitchen. He's already a giant wooden man. He doesn't need even more attention on him. Although, he will be with me—the invisible girl. Maybe our effects will cancel each other out. A heart-stitched apron hanging on the wall near a cabinet catches my eye. "Here we go." I tie the fabric around his waist, stepping back to take a look at my handiwork.

He gives a twirl, and I giggle. "Well?" he asks.

"It will do." I kiss him on the cheek and lead him toward the door.

***

I was wrong. I thought being constantly ignored and bumped into was the worst fate. Being perceived? So much worse. As Pineo and I walk hand in hand through the town square, my cheeks burn bright, and my skin crawls on the back of my neck. Every eye is on us. Mouths wide and whispering once they take in Pineo's wooden form. It doesn't help that he's so tall and handsome. Even if he was a normal man, I figure people would notice him, but now it's like he's a walking spectacle.

We were able to dip into the garment shop and purchase him a pair of pants, although they didn't have the right size, and his wooden ankles stick out. Now as we try to weave through the masses to the cinnamon roll stand, I fear we won't make it. Men and *especially* women stop us every few steps. They ask questions, smile brightly at him, and even touch his arms to feel if he's real.

I've never been a jealous person. There was so much I didn't have that if I was, it would drive me crazy. But now I know the true meaning of the word. As I watch a beautiful, busty blonde rub up against Pineo as she comments on how strong he seems, I can't take it. To Pineo's credit, he can't take his eyes off me. He never looks at the person speaking to him. He just searches me as my cheeks heat and I panic.

I pull away from the crowd, bustling off the cobblestone road and toward the woods. My heartbeat pounds in my ears, and I steady my breath, letting the quietness of the forest wash over me. It's not until I hear Pineo calling my name and stomping after me that I realize I left him in a place totally unfamiliar to him. It's a shitty thing to do. It's not his fault everyone is drooling over him. I can't help my broken heart, though. Watching him come after me, women trailing behind him, my heart chips. People will never leave us alone. Will Pineo really want me when he realizes how many other options he has? I was foolish to think this was the start of my happily ever after. This is just a dream I'm about to wake up from.

Chapter Four
PINEO

I'm out of breath when we close and lock Clara's cottage door behind us. I rest against the wooden wall. The chatter from the townsfolk dampens, but there's no mistaking that they're still outside. "Is it always like that when you go into town?" I say, out of breath.

"No," she spats, walking away from me and charging toward the kitchen. I can't see her face, but I've studied her all my life. I know she's upset. "What is wrong?" I ask, trailing after her.

She averts her eyes from me, opens a cabinet, and sticks her head in, pretending to rummage around for something. "Nothing is wrong. I'm just hungry."

Someone knocks, and I whip around to the people crowding the window, cupping their eyes to peer in at us. I rush to draw the blinds. "Maker, these people are wild!" I lean against the green fabric, my hand over my beating heart. Clara never returned home with a crowd like this. I look different, but I wouldn't have imagined so many people would be interested in me.

Clara whimpers, and I abandon my post and rush toward her. She darts from the cabinet before I reach her, and rushes down the hall toward her bedroom.

"Clara, where are you going?"

She shuts the door behind her but calls out to me, "I'm just tired from the day. I think I need to take a nap."

I jingle the doorknob. It's locked. "Can I take a nap with you?" I sound like a child.

"No, I just need to be alone." She tries to hide her whimpers, but it's obvious that she's crying. What can I do? Should I break the door down and demand she tell me what's wrong? That doesn't seem like something she'd like. She's always lived a calm and quiet life—without loud proclamations or confrontations. Maybe the crowd of people are too much for her.

My wooden heart races as my mind whirls with possibilities. Maybe my appearance embarrassed her in front of her peers. People seemed to like me and wanted to know about me, but maybe they weren't sincere. Perhaps she doesn't like the attention I'm bringing, and she's realizing there is no chance of a life with me.

A sob from Clara's room tugs at my chest. I can't bear to be the cause of her pain. All those lonely nights when she mourned for her father or begged the stars to end her loneliness, I wished I could soothe her. But now, here I am, capable of wrapping my arms around her and whispering soothing words, and I'm only rubbing dirt into her wounds. I'm the cause of her pain. Maybe she would be better off without me.

I turn away from the door, sitting on a chair by the unlit fireplace. I won't leave without a goodbye, but leaving could be the only way to give the girl I love most, the happiness she deserves.

Chapter Five
CLARA

Nothing makes you feel more well-rested than a good cry, stuffing your face with granola, and a heavy nap. There's a glimmer of happiness during my first blink of wakefulness, but then I remember the sadness that washed over me before I fell asleep. Now that I've napped and eaten, I realize I might have overreacted. I'm still anxious about Pineo leaving me for the attention of everyone else in the world. Still, I should have just told him my worries instead of barricading myself in my room and making a big production.

I don't know how long I've been asleep, and guilt riddles my consciousness as I crack open my bedroom door and peer out into the hall. It's silent. My heart drops at the thought that maybe Pineo has already left. Perhaps he decided I'm too dramatic, and he's already sick of our life together.

I race out of my room, taking in my small living space. Thankfully, it seems the people surrounding my home have left. I don't hear any chattering, and even though the curtains are drawn, I don't see the light shifting on the other side from people moving about. I sigh in relief once I spot Pineo asleep on a chair by the fireplace. Seeing him already makes me feel better. I crawl onto his lap, nestling into his neck. He wraps his arm around me, rubbing his fingers lightly over my skin.

It takes him a while to pull himself out of sleep. At first, he holds me tightly—allowing me to share his warmth, but as his eyes flutter open, his spine straightens. I gaze up at him from his lap. "I'm sorry I was so upset," I say in a small voice.

His hands fall from me, and I sense he means to get up. I crawl off him, confused and worried, and sit back down at the edge of the chair, staring up at him,

"It's my fault," he says, standing beside the chair. "I upset you."

I pop to my feet, grabbing his hands. "No, Pineo. It's not your fault. I just saw the way everyone reacted to you and..."

"Yes, I know. I embarrassed you, and I will continue to embarrass you. Look at me. I'm a hideous freak. My skin is made of wood, and I'm much too tall. You deserve someone that you can bring out and show off. You'll never be happy with me."

Blood rushes to my face. "Pineo. That's not true. I want to be with you. I don't care about other people."

"But you will. It's already become too much just from a short trip into town. Imagine a whole life with me." He turns from me, tears in his eyes.

I grab his hand. "Pineo, wait. Is this what you want? Can you live a happy life without me?" He's saying he's leaving to make me comfortable, but what if this is all just to mask the truth? What if all my fears are true? What if he tasted the sweetness of the attention and realized I would never be enough? My body shakes, but I keep hold of him. I can't let him go until I know the truth.

He turns back to me, studying me intently. It's like I see his brain working behind his eyes. I don't understand why this isn't just a simple yes or no answer. "Well, what is it? Do you want to leave?"

Finally, his lips part. "Yes. I want to leave."

My heart breaks, studying his face in disbelief. I hear a rip, and I'm pushed away from him, but not by his hands. I look down; his dick has broken through his pants again and grows impossibly long, much longer than before.

"Oh no. I'm sorry." His wooden face reddens, and he attempts to cover his member.

My mind races with the events that happened before his dick grew last time. He had told a lie. He told me that he didn't watch me pleasure myself, and his cock burst through his pants. Now, this time, he tells me he wants to go, and it happens again. Maybe it's my mind playing tricks on me—not letting me drown in my sorrow just yet, or maybe he's lying.

"Pineo, were you telling the truth when you said you wanted to leave?"

He's distracted by his massive cock, not meeting his eyes with mine as he tries to turn away from me. I wrap my fingers around his head, and he shudders, moaning with pleasure and his eyes rolling back into his head. I slowly stroke him, a small fraction of the length. "Pineo, are you lying to me?" I stroke lower, and he moans again, giving into my touch. "Yes," he answers through a heavy breath. "Yes, I lied. I thought it would be better for you. I'm sorry."

I tsk. "My wooden boy. It seems that your dick grows every time you lie."

His eyes shoot open, and I pause my movement. "Oh, I guess that makes sense. How foolish of me."

"Shhh." I walk closer to him so I can roll my closed fist down his cock to meet his body.

"Oh, Maker!" he croaks as I get closer. "That feels too good, Clara. I don't deserve this."

I press my body against him, rubbing my hardened nipples under my shirt against his chest. "You have only lied to me to protect me or my feelings. You don't need to lie to me, Pineo, but I know you would never lie to hurt me." I reach down and grab his wooden balls underneath his member. They're so large and swollen, heavy in my hand.

He groans, throwing his head back. "They're going to burst," he says.

I rise on my toes, bringing my lips to his ear. "I want your wooden balls to burst inside of me. I want you to coat my insides with your maple syrup come."

He sobers for a moment, studying me. "But Clara, I could hurt you. My dick is too long."

I trace his jaw, staring into his eyes. "What did I tell you? Stop worrying about hurting me. We'll figure it out together. We're a team. We just need to be honest, and everything will work out."

He nods. "Okay, but you must tell me if it becomes too much."

"Of course," I kiss his lips, and he parts for me, our tongues swirling together. I let my body melt into his, trying to enjoy the moment but also playing mental gymnastics around how this is going to work. I want his dick inside of me. We could wait until it returns to normal size, but what's the fun in that? The magical stars made his cock grow for a reason, and I don't plan on wasting their blessing. I stop kissing him, an idea popping into my head.

I rush to the kitchen, reaching to the high cabinets to grab the container of almond oil.

"What is that?" Pineo asks as he watches me walk back over.

I open the jar, sticking my hand in and scooping out a large dollop. "I need to oil your wood," I say, grabbing the base of him. He hisses as I slowly roll my fist down his length. I don't need to oil him all the way to his base. There's no way he could fit all of himself inside of me. I'd be split in two. But I love feeling his subtle vibrations under my fingertips as I lather him slowly, walking further away from him and closer to his tip.

When I reach his end, I turn to him, soaking in the view of him panting and struggling to regain his control. "Clara, it's too much."

"Don't worry, baby. We'll take it slow." I remove my hand from his cock, slowly pulling my shirt overhead and letting my breasts bounce free. My nipples are already peb-bled from the anticipation and the cool air pinches my skin. I rub my oily hands over my chest, my breath heavy as I gaze at Pineo, watching me and gripping the base of his cock. "So perfect," he whispers. "The most beautiful sight I've ever seen."

His words give me the encouragement I need. I shimmy out of my long skirt, letting the fabric fall to my ankles. My hands trail down my body, my cunt begging me to seek out its warmth. My lips part as I dive my fingers into myself. "I'm getting myself ready for you. I'm so wet. You're going to slip in so easily."

"I want to touch you," he says, his eyes dark and half-lidded.

"You have forever to touch me. Now you can watch and enjoy."

"I've spent my lifetime watching you. It's not enough anymore."

"Then I guess you're going to have to fuck me. Will that be enough?"

He moans. "Yes, yes. I need to be inside of you."

I'm officially soaking, drenching my hand. I'm ready for him and can't wait any longer for his wooden dick to be inside of me. I turn around, bending over and bracing myself on the wall before me. "Fuck me, Pineo. Impale me on your wooden cock."

I hold my breath as his tip meets my entrance—the movement slow and sloppy. It must be difficult to control such a long instrument from so far away from me. I crave his strong body folding over me as he pounds me from behind, but the opportunity to ride his inhumanly long dick is too enticing to pass up.

"Are you okay?" he asks, his voice shaking, barely able to control himself with just a small bit of him inside of me.

My body sings with the anticipation. I move my hips back to encourage him. "Yes, baby. I'm ready for you." He sinks in deeper, stretching me wide, but it's still not enough. I push back, squeezing around him. He moans loudly, and his shudder vibrates inside of me. "Yes, Pineo. So good. It feels so good."

"Too good. Too tight. I don't know how long I'll last."

"Go as long as you can. I want to see how much of this wooden dick I can take."

"Let me know if I'm hurting you, and I'll stop."

"Yes," I cry, desperate for him now, my inside walls shaking.

He thrusts into me, deeper, and it's barely a discomfort. I'm a virgin being fucked by an enormous wooden dick. It should hurt a lot worse based on how women around town described this act. He stretches me to a point of pain, but right when it builds, it blooms into a warm caress of bliss. I've never experienced something so wonderful. I push my hips back, eager for more, as much as I can take without being split in two.

"Clara, you're so tight around me. It feels like heaven."

"More, Pineo. More." He heeds my request, going deeper. I'm not sure where his body ends or mine begins. He's part of me now. My body makes room for him as if he's truly made for me in every way. I'm too lost in the pleasure, building, and building as he fucks deeper and deeper. It's not until his arms wrap around me and his breath warms my neck that I realize he's all the way inside of me.

I'm so deliciously full, but how is this possible? His dick was much too long to fit inside of me. It was longer than my entire body length.

"Your cunt," he whispers in my ear, running one hand over my breast and the other down my abdomen. "It must be forming my dick to your size. It feels so perfect."

Maybe this is part of the magic, too. Maybe my pussy has returned his dick to its normal length—one that gives us the perfect amount of pleasure. As if he needs to be any more perfect.

His finger grazes my sensitive clit, and I scream. Stars blur my vision. My blood evaporates from my body, and in its place, liquid lava flows through my veins. I've orgasmed before, but this is different. Holy, magical, enough to send a person to an early grave without regrets or wishes. Is this how fucking feels for everyone? How can anyone get anything done with knowing something so heavenly exists, just one dick away? It must be different. There is no way anyone has ever experienced such bliss, not even Pineo.

But he moans into my ear as if to convince me otherwise. "Clara, Maker! So good. So tight. I'm about to burst!" He thrusts one last, long, and hard movement, slapping against my backside. Warmness fills me as he slows his speed, moaning and groaning in my ear. I've already come, but it feels so good—my pussy milking him of every last drop of his delicious seed as if it's as hungry for the taste as my mouth.

The clouds clear as our breath returns to a normal tempo. I don't want to move—don't want this moment to end, but I need to make sure I haven't died on Pineo's wooden cock, and the rest is just my version of heaven. I straighten a tiny bit, snapping Pineo out of his trance. His hands grab my face, trying to turn my attention to him. "Are you hurt? Are you okay?" His eyes search me frantically.

"I'm fine," I say with a laugh. "At least I think I'm fine." I step forward, his cock slipping away from me. I hate the feeling. Sure enough, his wooden rod has turned back to its normal size. Still long, wide, and gloriously smooth, but not a six-foot pole. Thank God. I might have been a little delirious from the hormones. He definitely would have ripped me in two.

Pineo wraps his arms around me, pulling me close and tucking his head into the crook of my neck. "Clara, my chest—it feels so full. I don't know how to explain it, but I care for you so much. I always have, even when I could only watch you from my shelf, but it feels so much bigger now. I would do anything to make you happy. I want to be with you forever. No matter what."

I know what he's trying to say, even if he doesn't. After what just happened between us, fully giving ourselves to each other, I know the truth of my feelings. I've known even before he was a living, breathing wooden man. Of course, it was much more innocent when I was a child, but now the feelings are intense, deep, and overwhelming, and they are about to burst from my chest if I don't let them attach to something.

I hold him tight, tears forming in my eyes as I bury my head in his chest. "Pineo. I love you."

I feel his heart beating, steady and strong. He holds me back, examining my face with wonder strewn upon his own. "You love me?"

"Yes."

"Like you and your father loved each other?"

I burst into a laugh. "Well, kind of, but also differently. Yes, I loved my father, but I love you romantically. I want to be with you forever, to kiss you, snuggle with you, and to give every ounce of my pleasure to you."

"That's what I want too. My whole life, I watched the love you and your father had for each other. Yes, you're right. It feels different, but just as powerful. I love you, too, Clara."

At his words, Pineo's hands fall away from mine, and his feet float off the floor. I shriek, watching as he flies away from me, his head nearly banging the ceiling. A thick mist and sparkling lights form around him. "Pineo!" I call, terrified that the star I've wished on has returned to take him away from me. Maybe the heavens only wanted me to experience true love, but I'm not allowed to keep it forever. I'm terrified, but I vow that I will love Pineo no matter what, even if he's confined to his lifeless wooden form.

The fog thickens until it consumes him entirely. I can't see him at all. The cloud sinks to the ground, and I charge after it, desperate to know what shape Pineo has taken.

It takes a second for my heart to slow down and for the fog and my tears to melt away enough to assess the situation. I stroke Pineo's cheek as his sleeping form comes into view. I gasp, pulling my hand away and sitting back until all of him is revealed. He wears the same clothes—the plaid vest and the new pants we got him from the market with a new hole ripped through the crotch. He's the same size, but he's entirely different. His skin isn't stiff and wooden anymore. It feels like mine. I touch his chin again, just to confirm. Sure enough, I feel silky skin peppered with coarse stubble. I can't believe it. He's a real man.

I fold myself over him, listening to his beating heart as I cry into his chest. His hand slowly rises from the ground and rests on my back, stroking me softly. "Clara? What's wrong? What happened?"

I sit up, gazing down at him. "Pineo, you're real. You're a real man."

He picks up his hands, examining his new human flesh. "Clara, how is this possible?"

"It must be our love. We confessed our love for each other, and you transformed into a human."

His attention leaves his hands and focuses on my eyes. "I'm so happy. Now, I won't embarrass you."

My expression sobers. "Pineo, you never embarrassed me. I was worried you'd leave me. All the girls were drawn to you, even in your wooden form. You have always been so handsome. I was worried you'd realize you were too good for me and leave."

He sits up, cradling my face. "Oh, Clara, I only have eyes for you. You would be the most beautiful woman in the world to me, even if I were blind. I've known you my whole life. I only want you."

My heart bursts, I'm sure of it, but surprisingly I don't die. My blood still pumps through my brain, and my body still carries me to my target—the lips of my love—my Pineo. I kiss him as if it were my last, even though I know I will be with him forever.

THANKS FOR READING

Thank you for reading! If you liked *Hard as Wood*, please make sure to leave a review.

Want more of G.M. Fairy? Check out her other books...

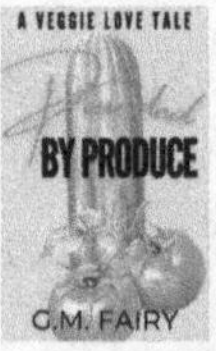

Pounded by Produce: A Veggie Love Tale

A tale of veggies tempted to break their vows.

Fleeing a tumultuous past, Emily finds refuge at a kitchen job in a quiet countryside parish.

Robert and Laurent are two best friends with a bond that has crossed lines throughout their history but now walk the straight and narrow, giving their lives to their parish as priests

One magical night under the harvest moon, Robert and Laurent experience a bizarre transformation: They wake up as a tomato and cucumber.

Emily brings these ripe and juicy vegetables into the kitchen, but instead of preparing a meal, she uses them for other, more carnal needs. Emily awakens something inside of the priests, who switch back and forth between their human and vegetable forms.

The three find themself in a steamy entanglement, unable to deny their primal desires. Will they fight their urges or break their vows and alter the course of their lives forever?

Get In My Swamp: The Completed Series

The three-part best-selling and viral sensation *Get In My Swamp* is now in one place.

Book 1 *Get In My Swamp*: When Liona stumbles upon Beck, the ogre's trap, and becomes his prisoner, she's determined to escape. But it doesn't take long for things to start heating up between the two. Beck is trying to protect her, and Liona can't help her body's reaction to the buff green monster. The lines between captive and captor become blurry, and the passion becomes a raging fire neither of them can put out.

Book 2 *Stay In My Swamp*: Life in the swamp can't get any better for Liona and Beck. That's until Beck pops a big question that forces Liona to face some unfinished business. She heads back to LA but Beck isn't too far behind, this time looking less like an ogre thanks to some help from Winston the Wizard. Will magic be enough for Beck to get Liona to stay in his swamp forever?

Book 3 and Standalone *Spellbound Seduction*: Winston the Wizard is a master of magic but a stranger to love. He has a full life in the hidden world of the magical community, but lives with a condition that makes it impossible to fully connect. He's content with his life as the manager of Happily Ever Endings, a club for adult enchantments, until he meets Marigold- a young woman who suffers from a similar condition, and she needs his help to take her on a journey to cure her curse. Winston feels an instant connection to her but knows they can never be. Can he resist temptation to keep them both alive? Or will he succumb to his urges and ruin them both?

The Crimson Wolf: A Red Riding Hood Love Story

Unearthing secrets, unraveling desires, and confronting the primal truth of the werewolf within the woods.

Red, a New York City journalist, returns to her quaint hometown to investigate a string of chilling animal attacks. Determined to unearth the truth, she reconnects with Jack, her childhood first love. The woods hold more than just memories, and a near-fatal encounter introduces her to Cameron, the infuriating and strikingly attractive park ranger with secrets as vast as the forest itself.

As Red delves deeper into the story, she unravels her family's cryptic past and finds herself entwined in a passionate and monstrous conundrum.

With her destiny in her own hands, Red must sift through her heart's tangled desires and the obscured truths of her lineage to discover the real beast of the forest.

Stay up to date on all things G.M. Fairy!